Rocco the

SWALLOWS THE MOON

Written by Rachel Smith and Charlie Ford

Illustrated by Jennifer Haslam

First published in the UK in 2020 by Smith and Ford, UK.

Text and illustration © Rachel Smith and Charlie Ford 2021.
All rights reserved.

Design © Rachel Hathaway 2021. All rights reserved.

ISBN: 978-1-9163488-3-7

Enquiries relating to reproduction should be sent to the authors at
info@roccotherockstar.com

www.roccotherockstar.com

Contents

Chapter 1
Elves on tour

"Elmer?" asked Louise softly.

"Yes Louise?"

"What do you think England will be like?"

"Well, I think it will be very green with lots of trees and castles and everyone will be very polite and offer us scones for tea," replied Elmer knowingly.

"Really?" said Louise, her eyes wide with excitement. "I can't wait to get there, it sounds amazing!"

"Elmer?" asked Louise, sounding a bit worried.

"Yes Louise?"

"Why are we stuck here and where are all the trees and scones?"

"I don't know Louise," replied Elmer gently, as he could tell she was on the verge of tears. "This isn't what I was expecting either, but Santa sent us here for a reason so we just have to trust it will work out."

"Chin up, Louise," continued Elmer, "and wiggle your toes or you'll get cramp."

"Come on, let's wiggle," he said, trying to lift the mood. Before Louise knew it, they were both wiggling and laughing.

Well, who have we here, thought Rocco – as nosey as ever – giving the Elves a good sniff. They don't smell like dogs and they don't look like dogs and they're not cats or humans. Rocco tilted his head to one side, looking at them quizzically. He looked at Sassie as she normally knew everything, but she looked as confused as him.

"Hey Charlie!" exclaimed Rocco's Mummy. "Look at these two Elves, aren't they adorable?"

"Yes they are, I wonder what they're doing here?" replied her friend Charlie.

"I'll go in the shop and ask," said Mummy, walking into the shop with Rocco following close behind her.

"Hello Rocco!" said the lady behind the counter. Rocco often visited the Charity Shop with Charlie when Mummy was at work. The kind ladies there always gave him a biscuit or two while Charlie was trying on hats and sunglasses and other random, brightly coloured things.

"Well, it's a shame really," the lady in the shop explained to Mummy. "A lady from Yelp came in the other day and she was complaining that the Elves were too big and she said she didn't want them anymore. She was actually on the way to the rubbish tip to dump them and

then she saw our shop and decided to stop and
drop them off."

Rocco's ears pricked up and he stood perfectly still.
Did she say the lady was going to take the Elves to
the rubbish tip?

Rocco knew what life on a rubbish tip was like – he
had to save these funny-looking creatures that his
Mummy called Elves. He leapt into action, dashing
outside and picking Elmer up in his mouth.

"Hey, where are you going?" Mummy called after him.

Charlie was outside laughing. "I think he wants us to take them home," she chuckled. "Come on, we'll buy one each, it's for charity after all and I don't think Rocco's going to let us leave without them."

"Okay," said Mummy, picking up Louise and paying the Charity Shop lady, "they do look very real and they are making me feel very Christmassy. On that note, shall we all go to Brook's for a hot chocolate?"

"Oh yes, that sounds like a plan," replied Charlie.

Rocco led the way, carrying Elmer in his mouth. He loved Brook's and he was keen to get in and see his friend.

Jasper was whining, staring up at Louise in Mummy's arms, wagging his tail frantically. "Oh, here you go Jasper," she said, "you can carry Louise. You boys are so competitive!"

Chapter 2

Chipping Dogbury delights

Later that day, as they walked back from Brook's –
getting some rather odd looks from passers-by it
must be said – they bumped into the Butcher.

"Good afternoon, Mr Butcher," Mummy said.
"Here we all are and we have some new friends
with us today."

Flo sat down quickly, stretching her neck round
the corner of the Butcher's shop to see if anyone

was around inside to give her a bit of meat. Rocco quickly sat down behind her, ever hopeful that something might get tossed his way too. Jasper joined in, as did Sassie, followed by Mummy's friend Elsie with her shopping trolley. Before long there was quite a queue.

"Oh my, I do hope your new friends don't start queuing for meat too," the Butcher chuckled. "I'll have none left for my customers."

"Come on gang," Mummy said, "I think we'd better head back home and let the Butcher serve his customers."

As soon as they got in Mummy found a nice spot for the Elves right by the Christmas tree. Placing them down gently she looked across at Rocco and said, "Now Rocco, leave the Elves alone and please leave the baubles ON the tree."

Rocco was really struggling to leave the tree alone, he couldn't understand it. It was covered in balls and what he thought looked just like toys, but whenever he went near it Mummy would shout, "Rocco, no, leave the tree alone!" Sometimes he just didn't understand humans.

He sloped off to bed ready to be tucked in. It had been quite a day.

"Elmer?" asked Louise later when everyone was tucked up in bed and they were sat on the lovely big, squishy mustard chair.

"Yes Louise?"

"This is nice isn't it, really comfy, and I can see lots of trees and green out of the window, like you said England would be. I wonder if we will get scones for tea tomorrow?"

"I don't know Louise, but this is much more like it. I wonder what Santa has planned for us though," Elmer said thoughtfully.

Chapter 3

P-a-r-t-y!!

Elmer and Louise fitted into family life with the gang with ease. Every morning Mummy would leave for work and Rocco, Flo, Elmer and Louise would gather around the Christmas tree and talk about their lives before they arrived in beautiful Chipping Dogbury.

Flo would always be the lookout, a job she relished and felt proud to do. As soon as she saw Charlie walking up the path to take Rocco and her out for a walk, she'd give a loud bark and they'd all resume their positions. Rocco would jump onto the windowsill and wag his tail excitedly at Charlie, Flo would jump in her basket and pretend she'd been asleep and Elmer and Louise would stand perfectly still either side of the Christmas tree.

One day, instead of everyone leaving the house as usual, Elmer and Louise watched with wonder as lots of people arrived with presents and balloons and cake.

Rocco and Flo were running around excitedly and Sassie and Jasper came up the path with a lady the Elves didn't recognise. They were all dressed up in their best clothes and collars.

"Come on in," Mummy said, beckoning to a long line of people walking up the path.

"Right everyone," said Mummy, "Charlie's just pulled up in her jeep. As soon as she walks through

the gate, thinking she will be taking Rocco and Flo out for a walk as normal, we will all jump out and sing Happy Birthday!"

"Quiet now, here she comes," Mummy whispered. "Flo, I know you were a guard dog, but this time you mustn't bark." Flo understood and sat quietly looking at the gate.

Rocco was taking the opportunity to try to find out how he could get to the cake.

Jasper couldn't see what all the fuss was about and Sassie was just so proud of her lovely Charlie.

The gate clicked, in walked Charlie and before she could get to the house everyone rushed out, singing:

Happy Birthday to you!
Happy Birthday to you!
Happy Birthday dear fabulous Charlie!
Happy Birthday to you!

Then everyone cheered and clapped. Charlie was absolutely speechless for once and Rocco thought she had a little tear in her eye.

"Thank you everyone, this is wonderful, what a lovely surprise," said Charlie.

Dylan, Charlie's nephew, was the first to spot the Elves standing by the Christmas tree.

"Hello, I'm Dylan, Charlie's nephew and this is my best friend Willow," he said to them politely with his loyal labrador by his side.

Elmer and Louise so wanted to say hi back, but they knew that they must never let the humans know they could talk.

"Ah, Dylan," Charlie said, "I see you've met the latest additions to our gang."

"Yes. Aunty, can we take them to the park with us after we've had cake?"

"As long as your mummy is okay with that and you go with some of the older children as well then I don't see why not," answered Charlie.

"Thank you Aunty, that would be amazing," said Dylan through a mouthful of cake. "Let's go gang!" he shouted excitedly, grabbing Elmer and Louise and tucking them under his arms.

As they crossed the road and walked down Love Lane, Elmer whispered to Louise, "Did you see that Louise? Only Chipping Dogbury would have a street called Love Lane."

Once they arrived in the park Dylan put Elmer and Louise on the swings and pushed them high up into the sky. The Elves felt like they were flying. Then Dylan carried them over to the top of the slide and pushed them down it, Louise's pigtails flying behind her. Rocco's schoolgirl friends Hattie and Eva Simone were stood at the bottom of the slide ready to catch them.

Then the girls plonked the Elves down on the park bench and went running off to join the others, who were jumping in and out of the stream and running around excitedly having lots of fun.

Jasper was looking everywhere for a ball and Rocco was desperate to get in the stream, but he was frightened of water. Well, he didn't like to think he was frightened, just cautious around it. Sassie and Willow were already in the stream splashing around and he so wanted to join them. He paced up and down along the water's edge giving out little barks of excitement.

Elmer and Louise sat on the bench getting their breath back and watching all this going on when they noticed a group of older children sitting on the other side of the park.

"Louise, what do you think they are doing, over there?" asked Elmer. "They look like they are having so much fun."

Flo, always on the lookout, spotted the group of older children. They weren't friends of Mummy or

Charlie and Flo knew to be careful of strangers, so when they started to come over she barked.

"Come on everyone, I think Flo is telling us it's time to go home," Hattie said, grabbing Elmer and Louise and leading the way out of the park.

Chapter 4

In with the wrong crowd

"Oh, thank goodness you're all back. It completely slipped my mind but the gang have their annual check up this afternoon at the Vets and then I have to go Christmas shopping. We have to go, we are late as it is," said Mummy as Dylan and the others walked in the door, all rosy-cheeked from their park adventures.

Everyone said their goodbyes and Mummy, Charlie and the gang hurried off to the Vets.

"Elmer?" said Louise when they had gone.

"Yes Louise?"

"I think while everyone is out we should go back to the park and see if we can join in with those older children. They looked like they were having so much fun."

"I don't know Louise, we shouldn't really go out on our own," Elmer replied anxiously.

"Oh, please Elmer, we need to learn all about England and the people in it while we're here," pleaded Louise.

"Okay Louise," Elmer sighed, "but we need to be quick to ensure we get back here before everyone comes home."

Once in the park, Elmer and Louise walked over to the bench where the older children had been sitting. To Elmer's delight there were a couple of cans of drink left and some leftover burger and chips.

"Can you believe this, how lovely that those children should leave all this on the floor and bench for someone else to eat and drink," Elmer said.

Elmer and Louise sat on the bench and drank from the half-empty cans and ate from the half-empty bag of chips left on the side of the bench. Elmer thought it tasted disgusting, but he didn't want to spoil Louise's fun.

"Who have we here?" asked a girl that Elmer recognised from earlier. The girl sat down between Elmer and Louise and got her phone out from her back pocket. Then she took her baseball cap off her head, swivelled it round and put it on Elmer and poking her tongue out she took a selfie of all three of them. The girl laughed as she got up. She grabbed what must have been her bike leaning on the fence and she was gone.

"I want to go back to the house Elmer," said Louise as soon as the girl was out of sight. "I don't feel very well."

Elmer wasn't feeling too good either and so he quickly led the way back to the house.

Chapter 5
Be yourself, Elf

Flo slowly walked over to Elmer and Louise as they both lay curled up on the floor at home feeling very sorry for themselves. She gently sniffed them all over.

"Mmm, you two had better straighten yourselves out by the time Mummy comes back," she said before slowly walking back to her rather comfy basket. She snuggled into it, giving out a gentle snore as she drifted back to sleep.

"Flo is so right," Rocco said. "What have you two been doing anyway to look and feel so dreadful?"

Elmer explained to Rocco that they just wanted to fit in and be like the older children they had seen at the park who he thought had looked so cool and seemed to be having so much fun. So Louise and him had copied them, eating and drinking like them but now they didn't feel cool at all they just felt dreadful.

Rocco listened intently to what Elmer was saying before he replied: "When I first came to Chipping Dogbury sometimes I would feel a bit sad because there were no other dogs that looked like me. Mummy said to me, 'Rocco you are unique and that makes you very special, there is no other dog like you.' When Mummy said that I started to feel very happy. So if I was you I'd just be yourself, Elf."

Rocco continued thoughtfully, "I don't know how to explain it, but when you are truly yourself it's like you've swallowed the Moon."

26

Elmer didn't really understand what Rocco meant, but he did like what he was saying about being yourself, Elf. That's what he'd do in the future, Elmer decided – he'd just be himself and then hopefully he'd never feel so bad again.

Flo suddenly started barking, snapping Elmer out of his thoughts, and swishing her tail at a frantic pace. "Yesssss, Mummy's home!" Rocco said, and both he and Flo ran to the door.

"Hello darlings, have you been good while I've been out?" Mummy said as she walked in with two bulging shopping bags. Flo and Rocco circled Mummy excitedly, both trying to get her attention AND peek into the bags. Rocco rolled on to his back ready for a tummy rub and Flo was doing pirouettes.

But Mummy was not impressed as she could see Elmer and Louise lying on the floor, legs and arms akimbo, and all the baubles from the Christmas tree strewn over the carpet. "Rocco, what have I told you about doing zoomies around the house?" Mummy said crossly. "You've knocked everything over. Really Rocco, you need to calm down."

Rocco felt very sad inside because Mummy thought he had knocked over Elmer and Louise, and he sloped off to his basket with his tail between his legs. "Oh, never mind," said Mummy, "no harm done, here you are, have a biscuit." She could never be cross with Rocco for long.

Chapter 6
A prickly rescue

The following day Mummy woke up and felt a little bit mean for telling Rocco off as soon as she had got through the door the day before. She decided they'd go on one of their special days out with Charlie and the gang and they could take the Elves for Rocco and Jasper to play with.

Wow, thought Elmer and Louise, this is so exciting to be out in the jeep with the gang AND it is Christmas Eve, the most important day of all for Elves.

The jeep slowly came to a stop and Jasper and Sassie started to howl with excitement. Rocco and Flo wagged their tails frantically as Mummy and Charlie started to put on their leads and gather up their bags, which were full of toys and treats for everyone. Rocco grabbed Elmer in his mouth and Jasper did the same with Louise and off they went.

Elmer and Louise so wanted to blink with sheer astonishment – this is just like home, they thought to themselves, just without the snow.

There were tall conifers neatly lined up, row upon row, the deep green grass and a lovely fresh smell of pine in the air. There was masses of green space, it was just epic.

Rocco, Sassie, Flo and Jasper sniffed and sniffed and ran in and out of the trees, while Mummy and Charlie followed behind trying to keep up.

"Come on gang, let's head to our special house, the Elves will absolutely love it," said Rocco, leading the way excitedly.

"Hey Rocco, is that you?" a man shouted from the
window of the most beautiful house that Elmer had
ever seen. In fact, was it a house or was it a castle?
Elmer wasn't sure, but he could see Louise looking
at him with eyes wide open with awe – in her eyes
it was definitely a castle, he could tell.

Rocco meanwhile was wagging his tail and running up to the window as he realised it was his friend shouting out to him – the lead Singer from the band he'd met once at a festival, the day he became a true Rock Star.

Mummy and Charlie went over to say hello, as they recognised the Singer too. He explained to them that he and his band were staying at the magnificent house while they were on tour.

The next thing they knew a lady came out of the very impressive blue front door carrying a tray with mugs of steaming hot chocolate on it, four bowls filled to the brim with warm, milky water and some homemade scones. Louise couldn't believe it, all her dreams of England had come true.

As it was so bitterly cold, everyone was very thankful for the warm drinks and scones.

The Singer of the band suggested that Mummy and Charlie should take Rocco and the gang to the other side of the woods where there was a rope swing. Rocco thought that sounded awesome, so they all said their goodbyes, wished each other 'Happy Christmas' and they were gone.

"What's all the excitement about?" asked Mummy, as Flo, Rocco, Sassie and Jasper all ran over to the same spot in the bushes, frantically wagging their tails.

"Wait!" Charlie said in a stern voice, sensing that something was up. The gang stopped in their tracks.

Charlie marched over to the spot. She couldn't see anything but she could hear a 'tap, tap, tap' noise.

"Come over here," she called out to Mummy, "I think there's something moving in the bushes."

"Oh, I see it," said Mummy. "It looks like an old tin can and it appears to be banging against that tree."

"Oh gosh," said Charlie, "it's a hedgehog. It's stuck in the can and it's banging against the tree. I guess it's trying to free itself."

"We have to help," she said, gently picking the can up and examining it.

Charlie turned the can upside down and carefully tapped on the bottom of it. Out popped the hedgehog. It staggered to one side and then collapsed in a little prickly heap.

"I think we'd better not leave it here," said Mummy kindly. "It looks a bit weak. It should be in hibernation now, tucked up warm, like all the other hedgehogs.

We'd better take it to the Chipping Dogbury Hedgehog Rescue Centre, Charlie, they'll know what's best for it."

So the gang did a quick u-turn and back to the jeep they went like they were on a mission. Rocco loved their days out, they were always so exciting! He'd never met a hedgehog before, but Sassie had. She told him to leave them well alone, as they might look like a ball but they were spiky and if he went to pick one up it would hurt. He smiled to himself, he knew she cared!

Thankfully they didn't take long to get to the rescue centre. Once there they were greeted warmly by a lady who had a good look at the hedgehog. To their relief she said, "This little chap will be fine, he just needs a good meal and a warm bed and he will gather his strength again. Thanks for bringing him in, not everyone takes the time."

"It's no problem," Mummy said, "we were worried about him."

"You certainly are busy here," Charlie remarked, looking around at the full cages everywhere.

"I know," said the lady. "We'd be a lot less busy if people picked up their rubbish so the hogs didn't get stuck in it."

"That's terrible," said Mummy, thinking to herself that she'd put up a sign next time they went to the woods to remind people to take their rubbish home.

"Well," said Mummy as they all got back into the jeep, "what a day that was. Our day out didn't go quite to plan, but what a lovely, happy ending." Everyone was looking back at Mummy smiling in agreement. They were all calm and quiet and a magical glow seemed to surround them. Even the jeep seemed to be smiling, but then Mummy realised she'd left the headlights on!

"Come on Charlie," she said, "let's go, it's Christmas Eve and we've got a lot to do."

"Yep, we can't just sit here grinning, homeward bound jeep!" said Charlie, being as silly as ever. Rocco knew the jeep couldn't *really* drive itself.

That evening, after their magical day's adventures, the gang went to bed early as it was Christmas Eve. Mummy said it was going to be another busy, special day the next day and they'd need their rest.

Chapter 7
A moonlight mirage?

When all was quiet Elmer and Louise took up their usual positions in the big, squishy mustard armchair by the window.

All of a sudden Elmer saw a flash of light and he nudged Louise, who had fallen asleep.

"Look Louise!" said Elmer excitedly. "There's Santa and his sleigh."

Louise jumped out of the chair and started waving frantically with Elmer.

"Santa, Santa!" Elmer cried. "Over here!"

"Hello Elmer, hello Louise, have you enjoyed your stay in England?" asked Santa as he brought the sleigh quietly to a stop outside the window.

The reindeer quietly munched on the carrots that the children in the street had left out for them.

"Oh yes, Santa, we've had a lovely time. The people here have been so kind and we've learnt an awful lot about England and castles and we've had scones and..." Elmer stopped himself mid-sentence. He was just going to say "and beer" but then realised he might get into trouble.

"And?" Santa asked, encouraging Elmer to finish his sentence.

"And," said Elmer, thinking quickly, "I've learnt that you need to be yourself, yes 'Be yourself, Elf', that's my new favourite saying."

Santa laughed. "Jolly good, that's a good lesson to learn."

Louise could sense Santa was about to leave so she quickly piped up, "Santa, do you think you could do something special for the people here? They've been so kind to us and we've had such fun."

"Well, Louise, as you know I'm very busy, especially tonight," Santa said, "but I hear your friends took the time to save a little hedgehog, so I guess I can find the time to do something kind for them. But now, my dear Elves, I have to go. I will see you soon back in Lapland. Take care." And with that, Santa was gone.

Chapter 8
A fabulous festive surprise

"Oh my gosh," said Mummy, running down the stairs in her pyjamas. "Come on Rocco, come on Flo, outside now!"

Rocco had never seen Mummy so excited and he couldn't help but join in the fun, frantically wagging his tail and practically pushing Flo outside.

"Can you believe this?" shouted Charlie, who was already outside with Sassie and Jasper. "It's snowing, on Christmas Day!"

Charlie and Mummy couldn't stop laughing as the rest of the street joined them outside. Everyone was in their pyjamas, running up and down in the snow, picking up snowballs and playfully throwing them at one another.

Rocco suddenly remembered Elmer and Louise and he dashed back into the house to get them.

Where are they, thought Rocco. They weren't by the tree, they weren't in their chair. He ran back outside to see if Jasper or Sassie had seen them, but they hadn't.

As he went back inside the house to have another look, Mummy followed him in and saw straight away that the Elves were gone.

Looking back at Charlie, who was coming in with the rest of the gang for a hot chocolate, she said, "What's this? There's an envelope under the tree where the Elves were."

"What's inside it? Open it now!" cried Charlie.

"Oh my gosh!" said Mummy. "Look!"

The End

"Enjoy the snow our dear friends in Chipping Dogbury and thank you Rocco - we'll always remember that the best thing to be in life is yours ELF x"

Meet the real Rocco and his gang of furry friends...

About the Authors

Charlie and Rachel are great friends in real life and meet regularly with all their dogs to go out in the jeep to far-flung fields in the stunning Cotswolds.

On one particularly amazing day out with the gang they decided to write a series of children's adventure stories inspired by Rocco and his rescue journey.

Their ultimate aim is to raise awareness of rescue dogs and to hopefully encourage us to be kinder to animals and each other.

In the spirit of kindness, where possible Charlie and Rachel work with and give back to dog rescue centres.

Other Books By Charlie and Rachel

Available to buy from
www.roccotherockstar.com:

Rocco the Rock Star

Rocco the Rock Star
and the Flower of Sascut

Rocco the Rock Star and the
Case of Mistaken Identity

Found a hog?

If you have found a hedgehog you believe needs attention, ask an adult to pick it up wearing thick gardening gloves, bring it indoors and place it inside a high-sided cardboard box, with:

✓ An old towel, so that the hedgehog has something to hide under.

✓ A shallow dish of water.

✓ A shallow dish of meaty cat food, wet or dry.

Then call the British Hedgehog Preservation Society for advice on what to do next.

If the hedgehog appears to be in a lot of pain or has a major injury, please take it to your local vets as soon as possible.